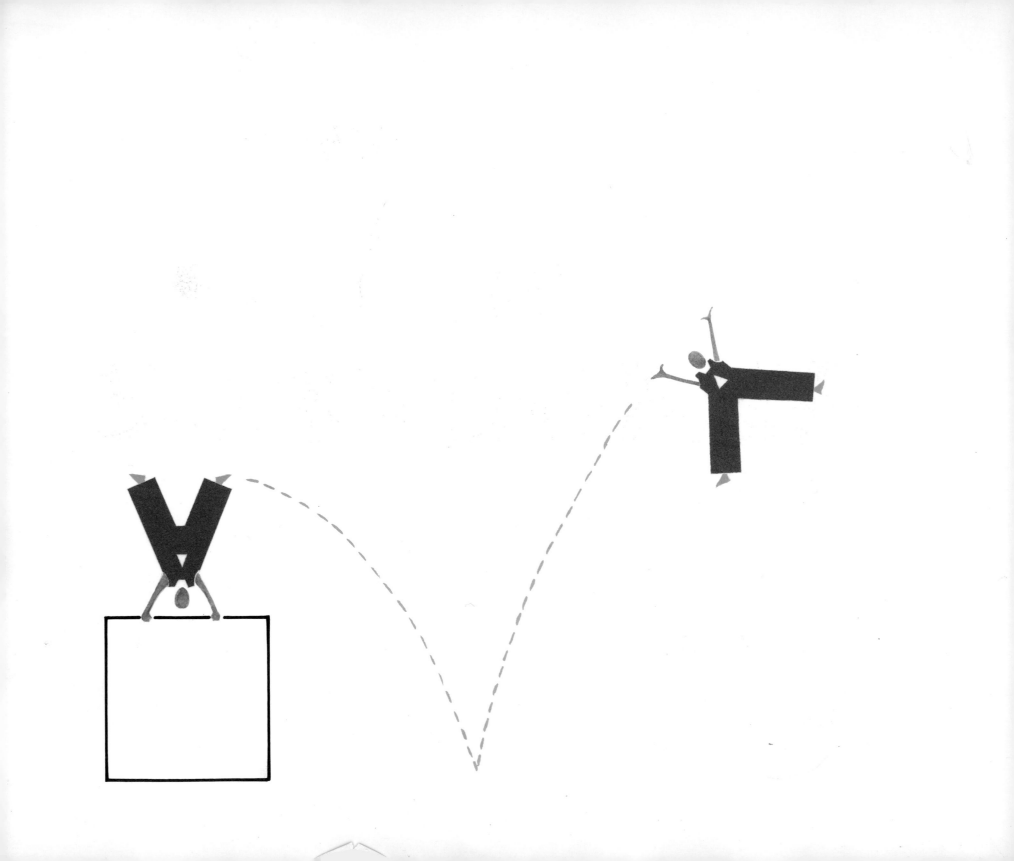

ALPHABATICS

Suse MacDonald

Bradbury Press
New York

Aa

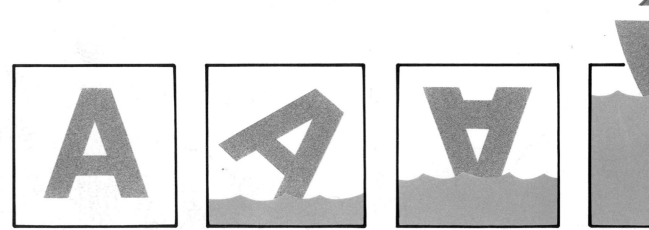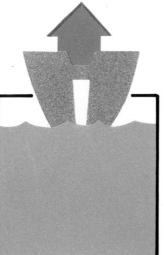

Ark

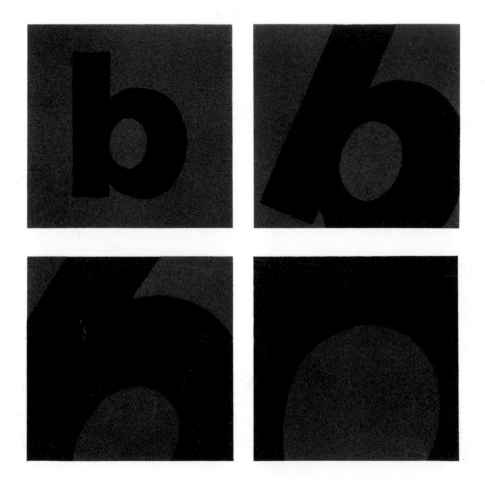

balloon

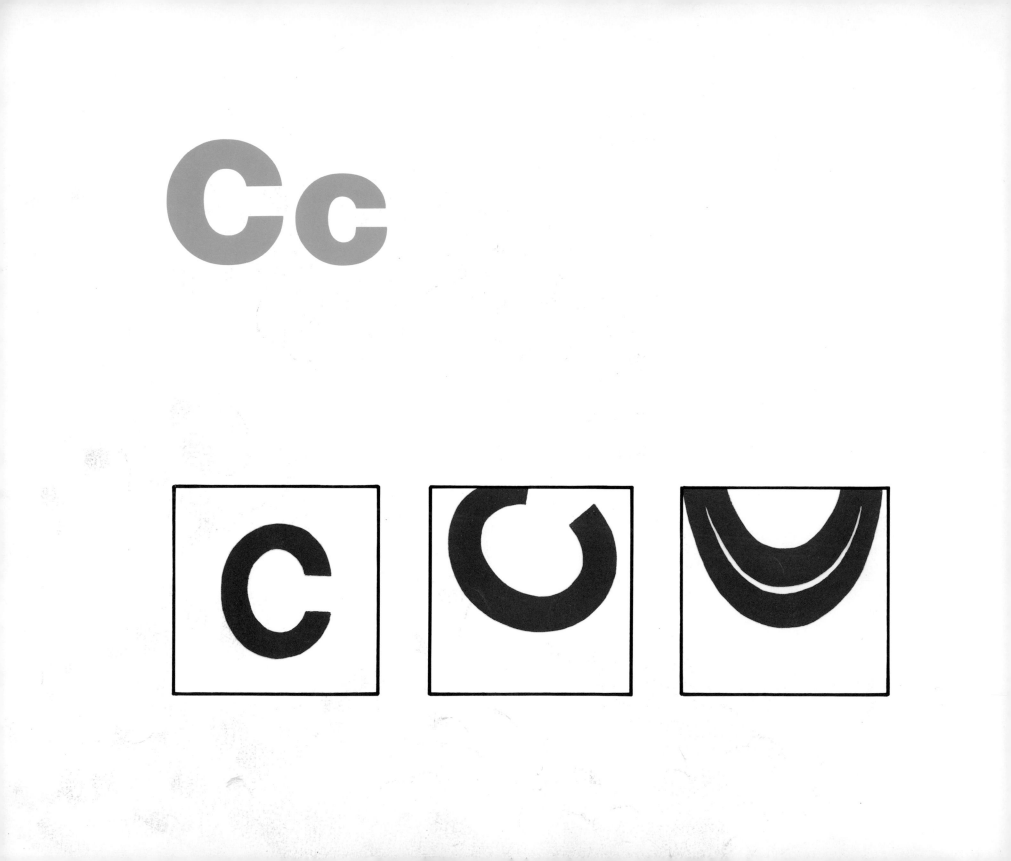

Clown

dragon

Ff

Fish

Giraffe

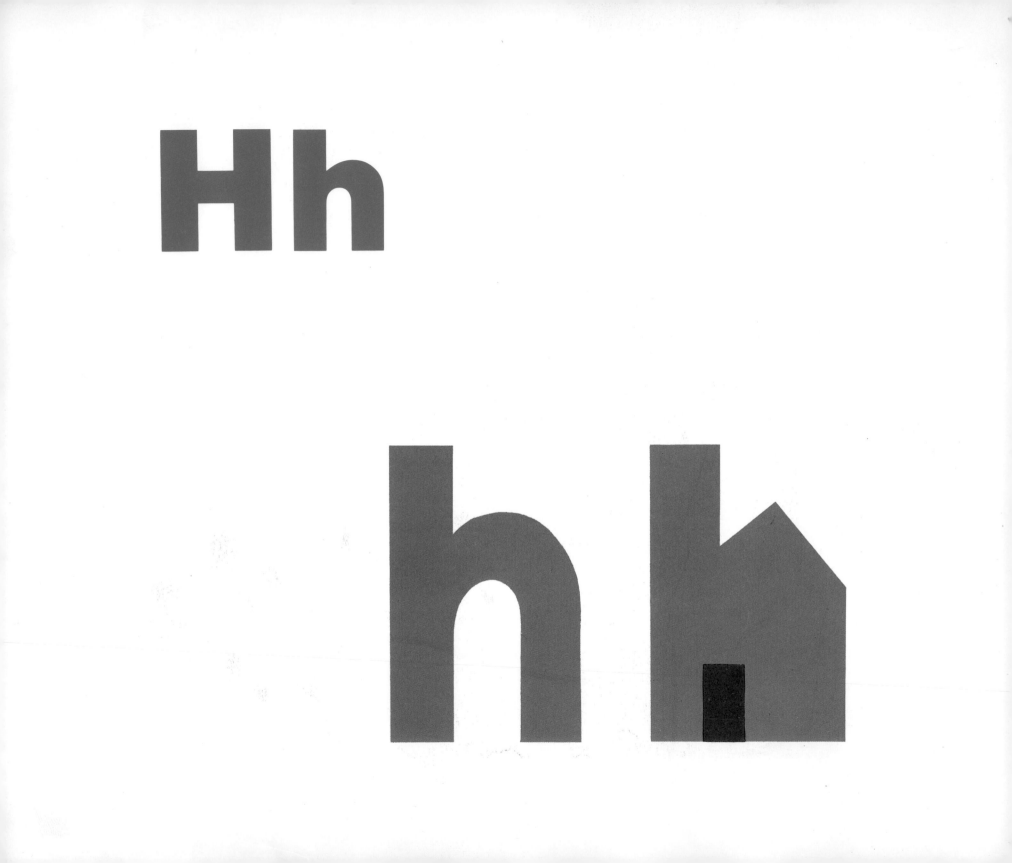

house

insect

jack-
in-the-box

Kite

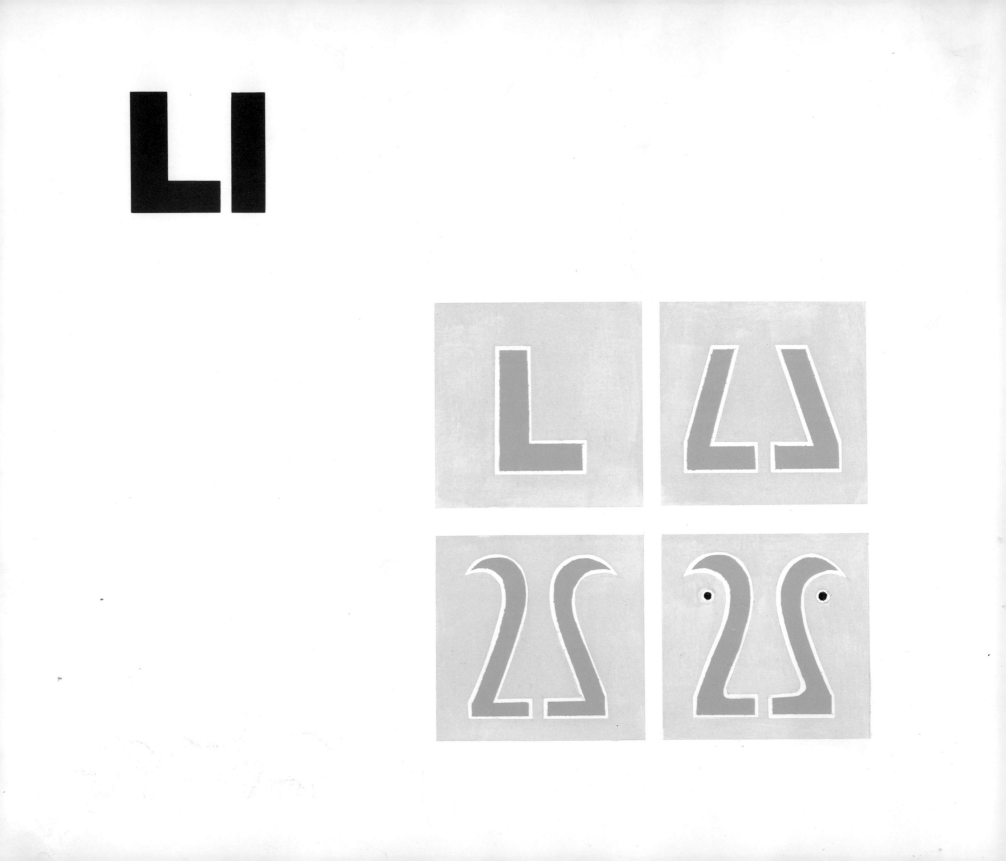

Lion

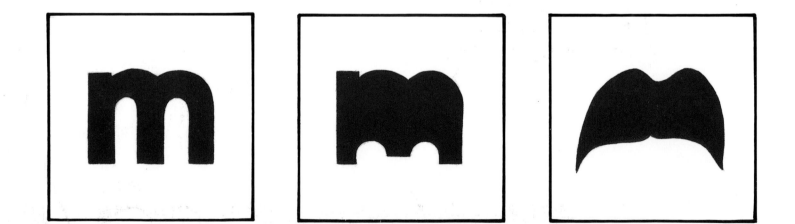

mustache

nest

owl

Plane

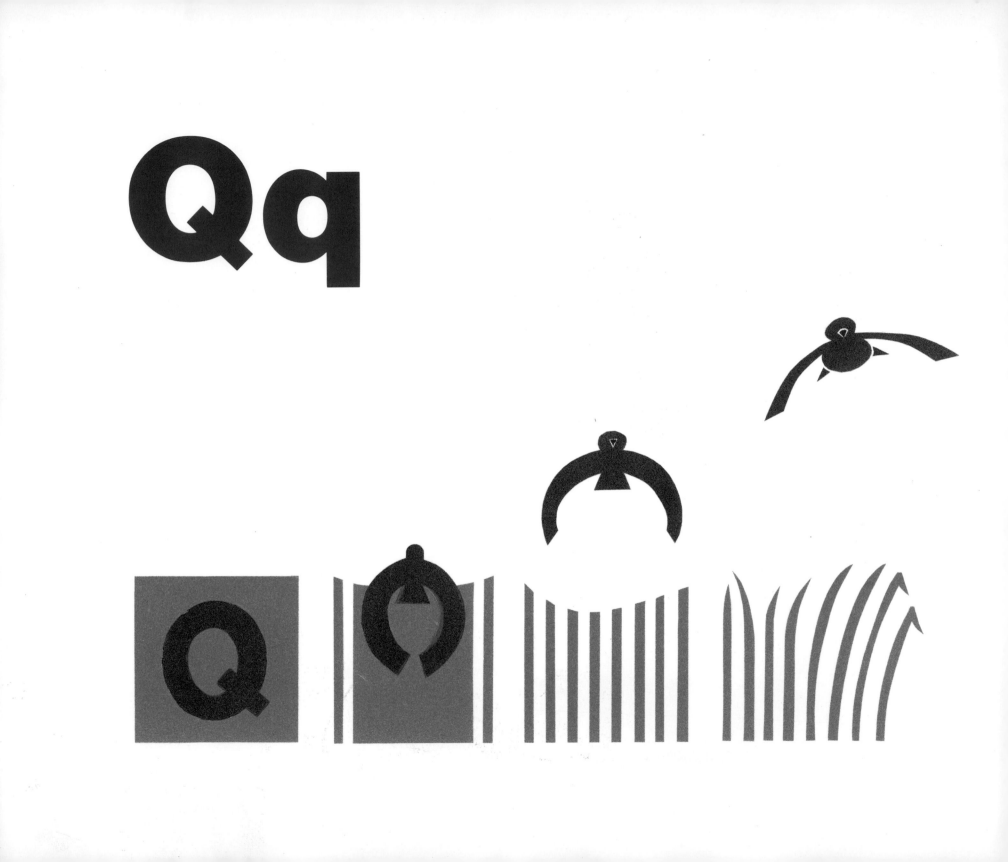

Quail

rooster

Ss

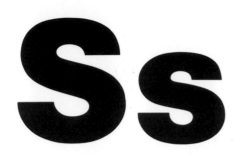

Swan

Tt

Tree

umbrella

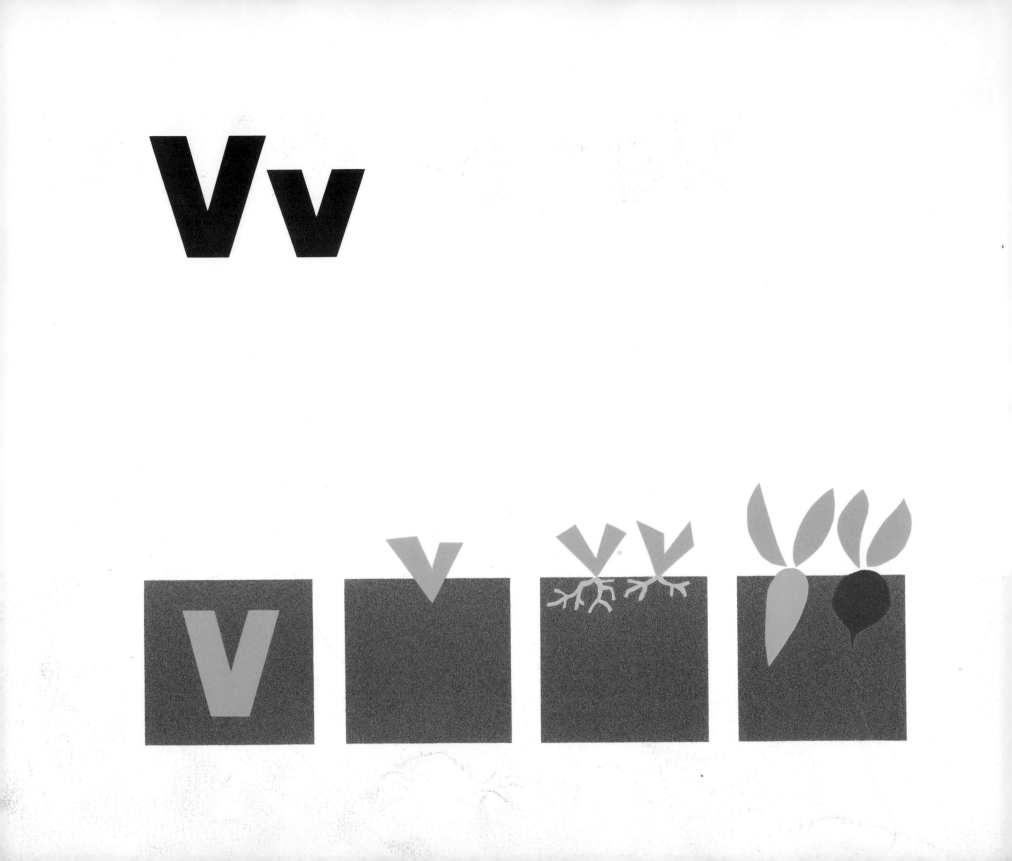

Vegetables

Whale

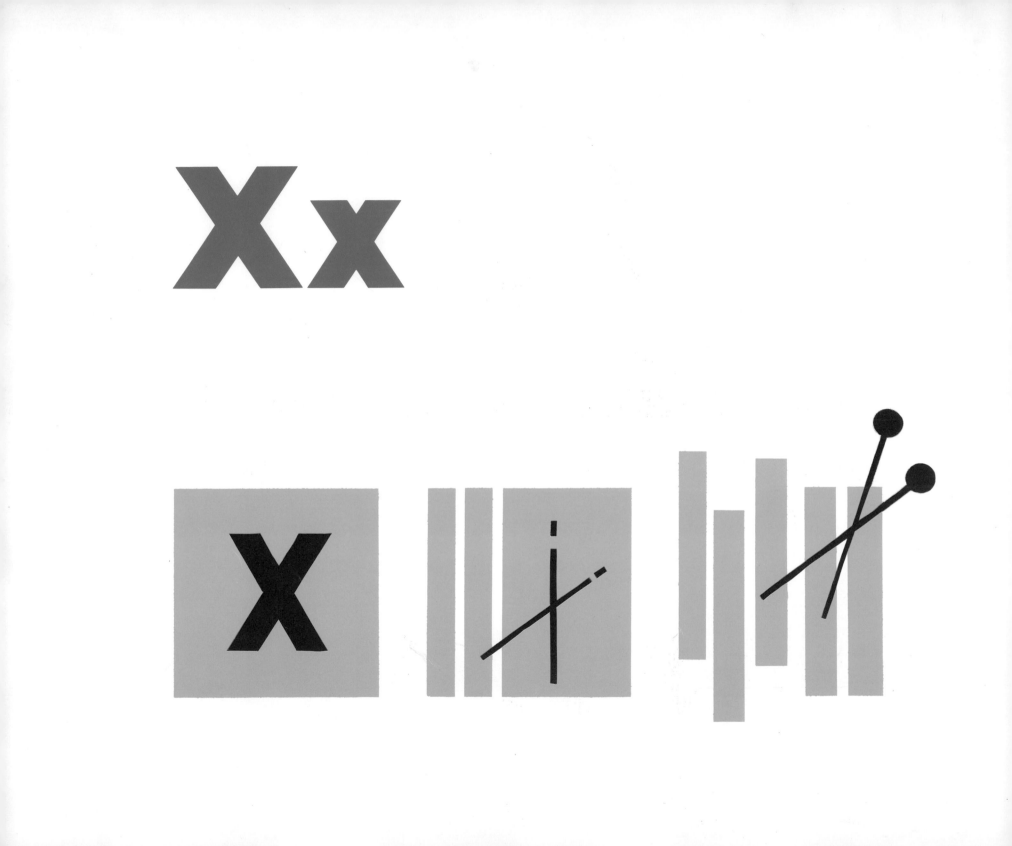

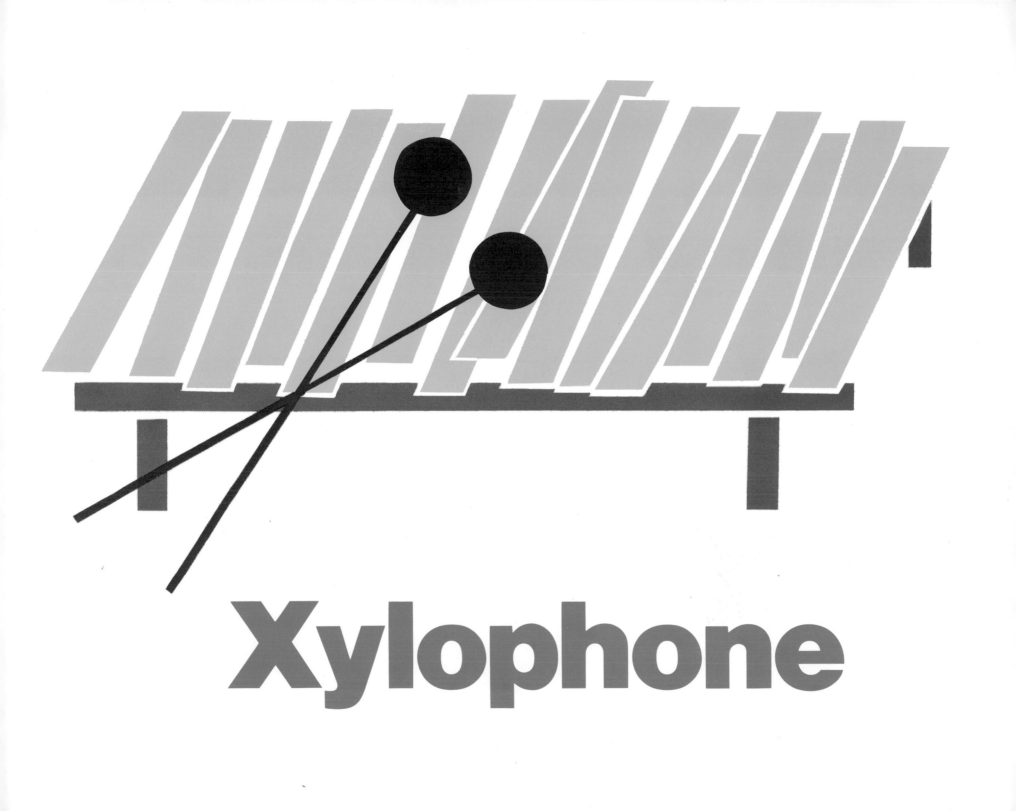

Xylophone

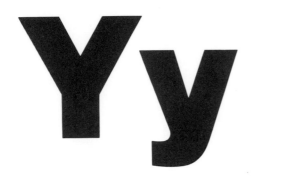

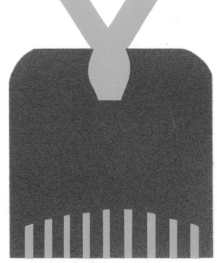

Yak

Zebra

For Stuart, with special thanks to Sarah and Deborah

1 2 3 4 5 6 7 8 9 10

Library of Congress Cataloging-in-Publication Data: MacDonald, Suse. Alphabatics. Summary: The letters of the alphabet are transformed and incorporated into twenty-six illustrations, so that the hole in "b" becomes a balloon and "y" turns into the head of a yak. 1. English language — Alphabet — Juvenile literature. [1. Alphabet]
I. Title.   PE1155.M3   1986   [E]   85-31429   ISBN 0-02-761520-0